# Baby Bear,
# Baby Bear,
# What Do You See?

## By Bill Martin Jr
## Pictures by Eric Carle

Henry Holt and Company · New York

Baby Bear,
Baby Bear,
what do you see?

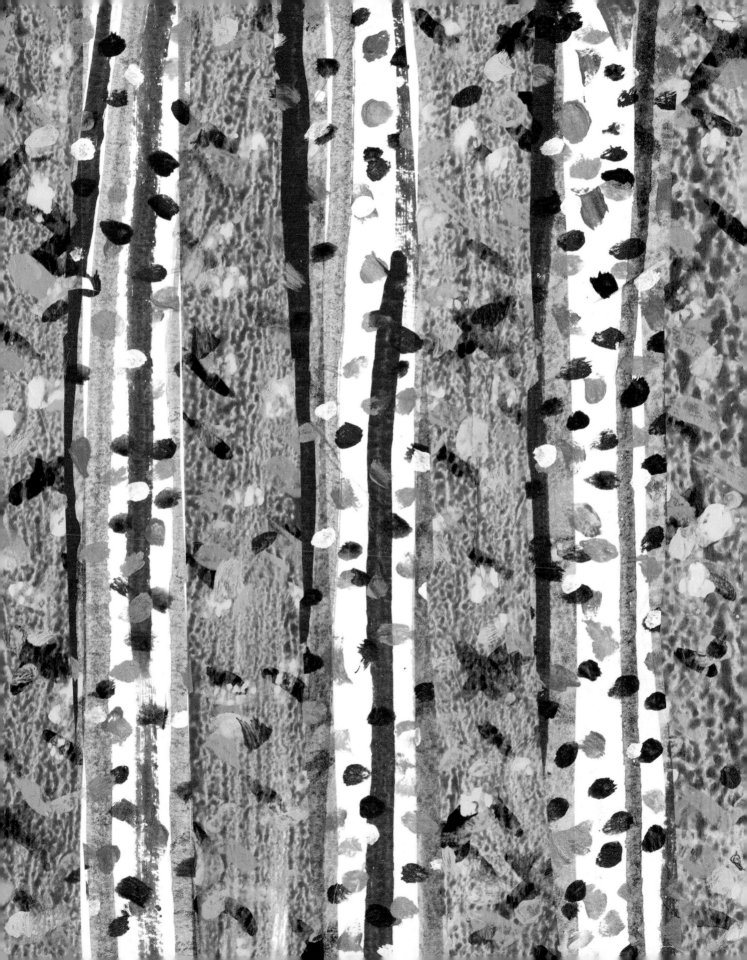

## Author's Note

North America is filled with thousands of species of wildlife. These creatures have lived in their habitats for centuries. Together, we can work to ensure that they will remain wild and free forever. This book features ten of these great American animals.

*The author wishes to thank Michael Sampson for his help in the preparation of this text.*

The Eric Carle Museum of Picture Book Art was built to celebrate the art that we are first exposed to as children. Located in Amherst, Massachusetts, the 40,000-square-foot museum is the first in this country devoted to national and international picture book art. Visit www.picturebookart.org

Henry Holt and Company, LLC
*Publishers since 1866*
175 Fifth Avenue
New York, New York 10010
www.HenryHoltKids.com

Henry Holt® is a registered trademark of Henry Holt and Company, LLC.
Text copyright © 2007 by the Estate of Bill Martin Jr
Illustrations copyright © 2007 by Eric Carle
All rights reserved.
Distributed in Canada by H. B. Fenn and Company Ltd.

Library of Congress Cataloging-in-Publication Data
Martin, Bill, 1916–2004.
Baby Bear, Baby Bear, what do you see? / by Bill Martin, Jr.; pictures by Eric Carle.—1st ed.
p.    cm
Summary: Illustrations and rhyming text portray a young bear searching for its mother and meeting many North American animals along the way.
ISBN-13: 978-0-8050-8899-1
ISBN-10: 0-8050-8899-7
[1. Bears—Fiction.  2. Mother and child—Fiction.  3. Animals—North Amercia—Fiction.]
I. Carle, Eric, ill.  II. Title.
PZ8.3.M418Bab 2007    [E]—dc22    2006037769

First Edition—2007
Printed in the United States of America on acid-free paper. ∞
10  9  8  7  6  5  4  3  2  1

I see a red fox
slipping by me.

Red Fox,
Red Fox,
what do you see?

I see a flying squirrel
gliding by me.

Flying Squirrel,
Flying Squirrel,
what do you see?

I see a mountain goat
climbing near me.

Mountain Goat,
Mountain Goat,
what do you see?

I see a blue heron
flying by me.

Blue Heron,
Blue Heron,
what do you see?

I see a prairie dog
digging by me.

Prairie Dog,
Prairie Dog,
what do you see?

I see a striped skunk
strutting by me.

Striped Skunk,
Striped Skunk,
what do you see?

I see a mule deer
running by me.

Mule Deer,
Mule Deer,
what do you see?

I see a rattlesnake
sliding by me.

Rattlesnake,
Rattlesnake,
what do you see?

I see a screech owl
hooting at me.

Screech Owl,
Screech Owl,
what do you see?

I see a mama bear
looking at me.

Mama Bear,
Mama Bear,
what do you see?

I see . . .

a red fox,

a flying squirrel,

a prairie dog,

a striped skunk,

a screech owl and . . .

a mountain goat,

a blue heron,

a mule deer,

a rattlesnake,

**my baby bear
looking at me—
that's what I see!**